U0074099

Poetry and Pictures

Francis S Cheng, Ph.D. ,D.Sc. & John Hsu, M.S.

A Tribute to Gifted Photographer

Mr. John Hsu, a gifted photographer, who likes to present water image rather than real object in his photos. Because it can show water image of sky, as outstanding background for desired composition. It also creates best painting-like photo, aided by water wave as painting brush. All photos displayed in this book are created this way. And the "Joy of Happy Company" is best example. Reader may view the original photo by turning it upside down, the scene will just look like common water image photo, not a picture.

Francis Cheng

A Scientist, Poet and Gentleman

Dr. Francis Cheng holds a Ph. D in Chemistry and D. Sc., in Chemical Engineering. He is a professor and poet as well. Not only that he is well respected, but also beloved by all of his friends. He is a genuine gentleman.

I have never met another Taiwanese in America, who is much courteous and gentle than Francis. And I feel deeply honored that he wants to write narrative poems for my pictures.

Francis is a science-oriented poet, who wrote about enzyme, planet and octopus in his poems. In fact, readers can find at the beginning of his poems, what he really meant to say, and this "Joy of Happy Company" poem is a wonderful example.

John Hsu

Contents

1 Joy of Happy Company

Mother Earth has eight famous sibling planets in company for four billion years.

Their sizes are from biggest Mercury, Venus, Earth, Mars, Jupiter, Saturn, Uranus, to smallest Neptune in solar system.

Each planet has their own mysteries and power of survival after undergone billion years of evolution and transformations in life cycles.

The key to survival may be having compassionate, loving, inspiring company, helping one another, and sharing fruits of success together.

2 Blooming Aqua Images

Spring breezes caress blooming forsythia by the pond. Florets spring off twigs, falling on water. Floating flowers collide with shadows on ripples, as if yellow sailboats jam into meandering river.

3 Dancing Rabbit on Cloud Nine

Blooming yellow flowers adorned the twigs, reflect with azure skies on rippling lake. All appears like white rabbit jumping off vase, hitchhiking the sailing, golden clouds.

4 River of No Return

Undulating streams flow down along meandering river. Azure skies greet splashing waves. Verdant plants wave goodbye to sweeping currents. Albeit streams look plain, life depends on them.

5 Coy Windmill

Invisible wind power is generated by air pressure depressions.

Air currents help windmill to come alive in water irrigation, power generation, and grain milling operations.

Image of coy windmill reminds us of ancient civilization.

6 Impish Cat Flees Fires on Water

Sparkling fountain casts ripple images of trees, housing array, and adjoining red tents as if fires on water.

Ghost image, impish cat is fleeing smokes in panic.

Even flocking ducks are diving to escape fires.

7 Camouflaging Octopus

Octopus is mollusk family similar to squid, which has no spine with eight tentacles; yet possessing nine brains and three hearts.

Each tentacle has its own brain for actions besides head main.

It uses three hearts to pump blue blood for two gills and whole body. Blue blood contains copper-based oxygen binding hemocyanin proteins.

Octopus can survive in, cold, deep sea, with ability to extract oxygen through gills and skins.

Octopus has color changing cells on skins, and muscle-stretch ability affords easy camouflage like menacing yellow dragon, innocent reef for fish playground, or spitting dark melanin ink for retreating.

8 Imaginary Fire Propagations

Flames ascend upward, and sweeping outward without boundary.

As if flue gas inside pizza oven was pushing away by turbulent flames, and heat fluxes of propagation reinforced from fuel and air currents.

9 Splendid Scenery of Digitized Painting

Breeze sweeps gently across the pond reflections, emulating vivid scene of trees and park goers, as if digitized oil painting.

The chrome, hue, and shade of colored objects are graded with numerical digits for art characterizations.

Smooth continuous, pleasant view of nature is artfully represented with lines and points of digital values, for perfect reproduction and lasting preservation.

10 Charming of Fallen Foliage

Pretty foliage signifies finale of autumn season. Their charms never last forever.

After two weeks leaves started to part, quietly plunging down, spirally landed on pond, forming mosaic green-drab islets for frog's jumping board, or protective mantle for spawning fishes.

Mother Nature cares about survival of human beings, animals and plants, recycling fading foliage using water, oxygen, and enzymes under the blessing of sun. Always keeping great earth safe, charming, and productive.

11 Spectacular Growing Weeds

Wild weeds pop up on land, riverbank and seashore – nature's marvel.
Their dynamic energy keeps them growing to greet the sun.
Green leaves swing in rippled waves as if waterfalls are seeking fun.
Vivid green leaves flaunt their charms amid cascading drab bundles.

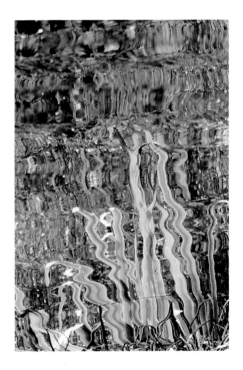

12 Sparkling Beethoven Image

Soft breeze brushes aqua image of yellow forsythia, painting sparkling curly-hair Beethoven, staring at piano for greatest No. 9, blessed by blue skies.

13 Aesthetic-Treasure of Spring

Colorful flowers usher the arrival of majestic spring.

Blooming of red roses, peonies, camellia, and pink campion greet the budding forsythia along meandering river. They are blessed by fleeting clouds in blue skies.

Water reflections of panoramic scenery appears as though hidden duckling, piggy, crane, and bear, being lost in floral maze.

14 Allure of Water Reflections on Fall Scene

Nature offers scenic colors to usher new season. Beautiful fall scene is most unique with kaleidoscopic paintings.

Water mirrors foliage images covering gamut of color spectrum to attest fall charms.

Nature's beauty is crafted by dynamic, powerful enzymes.

15 Kaleidoscopic Fall River Scene

Sparkling fall scene of reflective river heralds pageant show of fall foliage, white clouds, blue skies, and flaunting drab branches.

Mother Nature loves mosaic ensemble of things blending in harmony, aesthetically.

The earth furnished water, air, soils, trees, foods and enzymes to support lives and recycling the wastes.

16 Beautiful Scenery of Charming Spring

Happy spring rejuvenates after frigid winter, as if great nature has walked away from snow-white desolate landscape, heading into pleasant, verdant paradise.

Parents with kids and pets, venture outdoors, enjoying chirping birds, blooming bushes, and tree blossoms, like pageant show, along riverbank. Where they cast long shadows on gleaming ripple waves.

Spring is so beautiful and charming, yet very assuring in rewarding efforts in all aspects of life for reproduction and germination.

Spring comes back once a year as earth tilts, 23.5 degrees, near the sun.

The miracle of Mother Earth in creating great incubator for nurturing lives should be respected and not be tarnished.

17 Pleasant Aqua Images of Spring Sun

Soothing breezes usher spring's return with bright sunshine.
Drab drooping branches perk up, shooting new twigs into cold air.
Twigs sway in caressing breezes, flaunting their tender images.

Spring revives nature's incubator for young creatures, plants, fish, and birds. They grow in wild, enjoying pristine beauty and challenge of nature.

All living lives need sunshine in daytime, providing energies for surviving and activities.

After sunset, crescent moon rises in the night sky, giving exhausted bodies to rest for recovery and growth.

18 Memorable Departure of Charming Fall

Most beautiful fall scene lasted merely a week, as if finale of nature's pageant show.

Verdant foliage of dynamic growth in summer suddenly faded as victims of autumn.

The foliage changed colors from vivid green to variant rainbow colors, to drab-yellow, beginning to fall from trees.

The falling leaves spinning in midair against dazzling sun, likened frolicking butterflies, bobbing and ricocheting on sparkled water.

Water reflections of aesthetic fall scene signaled end of harvest season before the arrival of snow-storm wintry winter.

19 Nature's Sparkling Beauty

Mother Nature nourished zillion creatures in her cradle.

She never complained about daily chores of revolving to replenish fresh air, keeping lives healthy, happy, and flourishing.

Nature created four seasons conducive for reproducing and sustaining lives, in spite of geographic differences and severe weather patterns.

While most impressive sparkling foliage in autumn, decorating over northern mountain slopes, signified harvest season was coming to an end.

Nature's magnificent beauty was symbol of love, harmony and hope.

20 Pretty Lotus Sailing on Mosaic Skies

Breeze fondles beautiful lotus against mosaic, rippled waves.
Lotus bobs happily as if emerging from serene life.
Frog hops from lotus to lotus like ricocheting jade.
Lotus never stops bobbing, enchanted with caressing breeze.

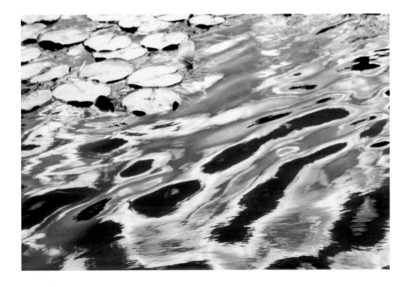

21 Splendid View of Green River

Dynamic green river greets parading admirers.

Splendid rushing stream helps irrigations, nourishing aquatic foods and plants.

The river water is nature's gift for survival and helps commercial transports for prosperity.

River is great attraction for tourists, yet vital for thirsty migratory birds.

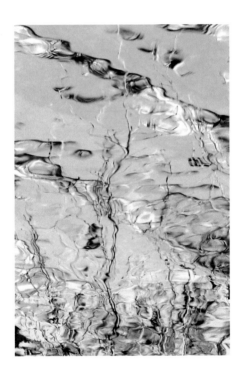

22 Nautical Pier Posts

Nautical pier posts queue for view. They are pretty yet sturdy.
Nautical pier posts stand on guard. Unfazed with high tides never get hurt. Day-in and day-out show no fatigue, as if flickering pool cues dancing under scorching sun.

Tall posts welcome visiting vessels as busy hosts. When ships are gone, rippled waves hugged them most.

23 Flag and Soldier

Flag stands for friendship, integrity, freedom, and trust of nation in world community.

Soldier guards the soul and will of people under sacred flag.

Valorous soldier never lasts forever, yet flag displays for eternal glory.

Soldier suffers trauma and sacrifice for the country.

Flag represents confidence, honor, and pride of great soldier.

24 Bon Voyage to Happy Cruising

Joyful rendezvous of ships and boats are greeted with partly overcast.

Blue skies try to offer sparkling panoramic view of ocean guests, while moody clouds are eager to give them refreshing showers at best. The sun is peeking behind sailing clouds.

Now ships and boats are ready to steam away. Cruising passengers are blessed with happy sailing under spectacular blue skies, with rising horizons at high sea.

25 Water Reflection of Heroic American Flag at Sea

American flag, spirit of people. Unfurls at turbulent sea, against approaching hurricane. Red sails are flaunting in mid air.

Greeting heroic flag, which tirelessly fights inclement weather for direction in reaching destination.

26 Marine Crew

Marine crew must be tough with wit when boat stalled on voyage. Oftentimes at night sailing, through estuary in ebbing tide, strong rip tide occurs, wrecking vessel off course, damaging jetty or pier without mercy. Good crew discerns danger, avoiding boat being pulled under.

27 Set Sail for Long Journey

Glaring sunset gleaming on the sound sent off ocean liner from home port for trans-ocean voyage.

Masterly captain and courageous crew were eager to embark on long journey at sea.

Perfect departure weather did not guarantee for smooth sail in light of severe climate change over raging seas.

The crew members kept vigilance, while navigating through the turbulent seas of terror, for safely reaching a foreign port.

28 Job Done at Gleaming Sunset

Time sails purposefully as Earth revolves.
Mighty Sun casts shadows on great Earth.
Workers strive to finish groundwork at pier before darkness.
Surging tides and sea breeze temper sunshine warmth.
Workers hurry to send off, gleaming, sinking Sun upon job done.

Poetry and Pictures

作　　者／許昭彥、程聖雄

出版策劃／獵海人

製作銷售／秀威資訊科技股份有限公司

　　　　　114 台北市內湖區瑞光路76巷69號2樓

　　　　　電話：+886-2-2796-3638

　　　　　傳真：+886-2-2796-1377

網路訂購／秀威書店：https://store.showwe.tw

　　　　　博客來網路書店：https://www.books.com.tw

　　　　　三民網路書店：https://www.m.sanmin.com.tw

　　　　　讀冊生活：https://www.taaze.tw

出版日期／2021年8月

定　　價／200元